Bella ButterFly
Lost in the Big City

Dear Baby Cirucci,

May you always be brave enough to fly!

Butterfly Kisses,

Lisa Satira Brozek

Lisa Satira Brozek

Illustrated by Mary Connors

AuthorHouse™
1663 Liberty Drive
Bloomington, IN 47403
www.authorhouse.com
Phone: 1 (800) 839-8640

Published by AuthorHouse 04/15/2015

ISBN: 978-1-5049-0223-6 (sc)
ISBN: 978-1-5049-0224-3 (e)

Library of Congress Control Number: 2015904386

Print information available on the last page.

Any people depicted in stock imagery provided by Thinkstock are models,
and such images are being used for illustrative purposes only.
Certain stock imagery © Thinkstock.*

This book is printed on acid-free paper.

authorHOUSE®

Bella Butterfly was as sweet as can be. She was the smallest of the children; in all, there were three.

Her family moved from Italy just a few months ago and settled in Pittsburgh where the three rivers flow.

Two older brothers were much bigger and braver. If Bella was in trouble, they always would save her.

Brother Antonio was blue with large, yellow spots. Brother Carlo was orange with green polka dots.

Mama was lovely in her pinks and her blues. Papa had stayed in Italy, sick with the flu.

Bella shimmered in silver and gold. She was the most beautiful; that's what she was told.

The family settled in their new and comfortable nest. As far as Bella was concerned, it was the absolute best!

"Time to go shopping," Mama announced one day. "You must listen closely to the words that I say."

The children gathered around, waiting for Mama's next words, paying attention to everything they heard.

Mother said, "Children, do not wander or roam; the city is large and very far from our home.

"You must stay close by, just an inch from my wing; and if you get lost, just whistle or sing."

They all got ready for their journey that day; each one was excited as they fluttered away.

Flying over trees, gardens, and flowers, they smelled the hint of a light spring shower.

How happy they were on their way to the city. It was just up ahead and looked oh, so pretty.

With so much to look at, Bella was really amazed; no one would notice if she wandered or strayed.

So Bella didn't keep up with her brothers; flying slightly behind, she disobeyed her mother.

Up into the air they soared so high. But when Bella looked down, she started to cry.

"Oh, Mother, I'm dizzy. I fear I might faint!"

She fell from the sky into a large pot of paint!

Sticky and gooey, she thought she might drown. Sputtering and fluttering, she fell to the ground.

When she looked up, all she could see were Mama and her brothers flying over the trees.

She tried to whistle, she tried to sing, but all that came out was a paint bubble ring!

She straightened up and shook her wings. Seeing her image in a window, she began to scream!

She was no longer gold, silver, or anything in between. What she saw was an ugly pea green!

"Mama Mia," her mama screamed. "My little Bella is nowhere to be seen."

Carlo and Antonio searched all over town. She must be somewhere, and she must be found!

Mama called Papa to give him the bad news. Papa said he would be there since he was over the flu.

Papa packed his bags and was on his way; he had a long trip to make that day.

Bella wandered through the streets of town. Hungry and tired, she just wanted to lie down.

Bella walked the best she could, since she couldn't travel by air. Her wings were all sticky. This just wasn't fair!

"I should have listened to Mama; she knows what is best. Oh, how I wish I wasn't in such a terrible mess."

Bella looked around town. Everyone else had gone home. Bella was in the big city all alone!

The streets were empty—it was quiet and still. Bella's stomach felt funny; she was feeling quite ill.

She started to shake, she started to shiver, and then her chin began to quiver. "I will not be afraid; I will not live in fear." Then her eyes filled up with big, salty tears.

"I must find shelter, for it will be dark soon. How I wish I were home in my own comfy room."

She walked along the streets, not knowing where to go; poor Bella roamed around for an hour or so. With a beautiful park just up ahead, she decided that was where she would make her bed.

She snuggled down under some beautiful daises. She was feeling tired and a little bit lazy.

Bella looked up to the sky; it was a lovely night. The stars were shining; the moon was bright. Bella felt safe and not afraid anymore. She fell asleep and started to snore.

Bella woke up to the sun peeking over the trees. It was a lovely morning as far as she could see.

Stretching out her wings and letting out a sigh, she sang so sweet and oh, so high.

But Mama and Papa had searched for Bella all through the night. They looked everywhere, but she was nowhere in sight.

When they flew over a park with many tall trees, they heard a faint sound floating up with the breeze.

Papa knew it was Bella. He knew the sound of her song. He didn't have to look; Papa never was wrong.

But when he looked down, he saw a butterfly of green—the ugliest green that he had ever seen!

Papa said, "Hello, my beautiful Bella butterfly."

When she heard him, she started to cry. "Oh, Papa, I've missed you, and I love you so much. How did you know it was me wearing such ugly green yuck?"

"It's not the color of your wings that matters as much as the hearts of the people whose lives you touch. Your beauty inside always shines through—that's how I found you, and I'm so proud of you!"

The family flew off to their cozy little nest for a warm bubble bath and some much needed rest.

Bella was happy to be back and safe at home. She promised her Mama she would never wander or roam.

Bella had learned her lesson and knew Mama was right. It is best to stay close and never fly out of sight.

About the Author

Lisa Satira Brozek is from North Huntingdon, Pennsylvania, and is the proud mother of two children, Caitlin and Christopher. She is excited to publish her first children's book, which was inspired by the memory of her grandfather, Giovanni Salvati. When she is not busy writing, Lisa enjoys painting specialty wine glasses, baking, photography, and spending time with family and friends.

About the Book

Bella is a beautiful butterfly from Italy. After moving to a new city with her family, she gets lost during a shopping trip and is forced to survive the night alone. In the process, Bella learns life lessons about listening to her parents, dealing with her fears, and realizing that the color of her wings is not as important as the beauty inside of her.

CPSIA information can be obtained
at www.ICGtesting.com
Printed in the USA
BVOW05s1558010218
506913BV00002B/3/P